If You Don't Like My Hair
...Just RELAX!

Copyrighted 2014 by Keke Chanel
Edited By: Shemica S. Huff
Cover Design: Keke Chanel
Image By: Liah Amori

ISBN-13: 978-0692239162
ISBN-10:   0692239162

This book is dedicated:

"To all the little girls in the world who are forced to live in the ranks of society. Be your own person! Love yourself! Embrace your natural beauty! Beauty is not about having relaxed or natural hair, rather instead by accepting that it's deeper and it is in the eye of the beholder. Don't ever allow anyone to make you feel inferior. You are more than that..."

Acknowledgements:

First, I want to thank **God** for putting this book in my spirit to release it. We often times come to a point in our lives that we become lost, unfocused and feel inadequate, especially among our peers. It's hard living in a world where people think that looking a certain way, acting a certain way, or living a certain way determines your social status and acceptance. We give power to the people who don't really matter! Why? It's simple. **WE WANT TO FIT IN!!! WE WANT TO FEEL NORMAL!!! Tell me, what is normal, exactly? (Take your time...I'll wait.)**

A special thanks to my daughter for allowing me to use her photo for my cover. **Liah,** you are an inspiration to me in more ways than you can ever imagine. May your light continue to shine brighter. I cannot wait to experience your accomplishments with you. I know that you will achieve everything you set your heart to do. God blessed me abundantly when He gave me you! **Louis,** son I am so sorry I cut your beautiful hair. (I kept your plaits. I have them. You just wouldn't let me comb your hair. What was I supposed to do?) **Bae,** sorry you stopped growing your hair in your twenties. I simply love your baldheadedness. ☺

To my two sisters Shan and Erica, my nieces Kiya and Ziggy, **"Natural Girls Rock!"** (Step into the natural Kemia).

To my other **family** and **friends,** thank you again for always supporting me and being my rock.

Thank you to all of my **Naturalistas** out in the world. You are amazing, beautiful, and to be cherished. Different is God's way of setting you apart; love yourself!

To **Allison** from **A Natural Hair Community** and **Kiera** and **Michelle** from **H2BN,** thank you ladies so much for being a part of my life. We have known each other for only a short time, but have become family. I am grateful to have you. Your products are amazing!

Purple Hugs & Kisses
Keke Chanel

Forward By: My Daughter

This book is special to me for many reasons. I, like far too many young, black females, know what it is to feel inferior in a society that tells us we are not beautiful because of the textures growing from our scalps (among other things). I have had perms, weaves, and felt the scorch of a straightening comb meant to tame what God created to be wild, thick, and free. I am done with those things. Going natural was not something I thought about until my mom began to talk about her own hair journey. My eyes opened. I realized that I did not have to continue to subject myself to the chemical burns, nor the constant fear of humidity ruining all the efforts of my flatiron. Prior to this revelation, I did not think I had a choice. Relaxers were all I had known. I did not hate my hair, but I have always felt more myself whenever I wear it in curls. As cliché as it may sound, I felt free.

I told my mom I wanted to go natural. By this time, the "natural hair movement" was in full swing. She told me I could wear protective hairstyles (i.e. buns, twists, braid, etc.) while waiting for the perm to "grow out" of my hair. Then, it seemed as though it would take forever. I just wanted to snap my fingers and have a huge magnificently fabulous Erykah Badu fro! However, all good things take time. As the months went by, I'd find myself standing in front of the mirror inspecting the roots of my hair. They were small and tightly coiled, but the curls were definitely there. They grew like weeds. I loved every moment. Yet, I secretly worried about what others would say, especially the people I went to school with. I wore my hair in a bun, afraid to release it for fear of being ridiculed. Sure, there were a few natural girls walking the hallways, but they had always been known for their natural hair. I had always had long, thick, *straight* hair. In short, I would not go undetected if I let the curls breathe.

One day I decided that I didn't care anymore. If girls could walk around campus with fire engine red hair or thick, blonde booty braids, I could walk around campus with my *kinky mane* let loose for everyone to see. So I did it. Can you believe I received more compliments as my **complete** *natural* **self,** than I had in all the years I'd been exposed to the "creamy crack"? I felt *liberated.* I felt *regal.* I felt *beautiful.* I felt **completely** *free,* not just hanging on the precipice. I wake up every morning that God so graciously allows me to see, and thank Him for blessing me with a supportive mother. A mother intent on teaching me that *my beauty* **is what** *I* **say it is, not what the world screams at me from all sides and angles**. I thank Him for molding me each and every day to know that I am a wonder. Going back to what he formed me in the womb to be was one of the best decisions I have ever made.

To the young girls who might stumble upon this book one day, please know that you do not have to depend on others to classify you plain, paltry, or pretty. Their validation will not bring you happiness or peace. Be you unapologetically as a gift. If they do not accept you, do not count their departure as a loss. It is for the best. Remember to love yourself and your body in all its imperfect glory. You only get one. **Walk upright and be proud** *like a princess* **soon to become a** *QUEEN*.

With love
Liah

"Once you go natural
Your mindset
Should also change.
Otherwise,
Your mind is
Still living
The L.YE!!!!!!!!!!!"

--Jazzyrock

Table of contents:

"If You Don't Like My Hair
...Just RELAX!"

Prologue

I still cannot believe it! It has been many years since I decided to *"go natural"* as many people call what I did; what many people call a trend, fad, or the "it" thing to do nowadays. How can you *"go natural"* when you were born that way? Hair without chemicals, just beautiful, curly, kinky, unprocessed hair; hair undamaged or manipulated by what society deems acceptable. We were not born into this cruel world perfect with flowing hair and beautiful skin. We were innocent. We were care free. The only natural things we had to do are eat, poop, and sleep only to wake up and do it all over again, Harmony thought reminiscing about her life.

I am now comfortable enough within myself to share my journey. It was not easy, but I made it. Thank God!

All the sleepless nights I cried because my scalp hurt so badly from the *chemical burns*. My mother never cared. As long as her little girl had what she referred to as *"good hair"* that she could brag about with her friends, she didn't care about the emotional damage I was experiencing.

I wanted to become a bird and fly away. I wanted to pull out all of my hair and disappear. *I wonder if she or anyone else would have noticed if I had gone missing.* Well, maybe my father. He loves me no matter what. Every child, especially a girl needs the unconditional love of her father. It can help make life easier. Unfortunately, my dad was so wrapped up with my mother and her hateful tactics, he did not pay too close of attention to the things I suffered through even though we lived in the same household. It wasn't always that way. In the beginning he would notice. He would even try to talk to my mother about her harshness. That only gave way to the problems they later encountered. Thankfully, they got their act together and are now still married, happily married. It still doesn't ease the pain I went through.

No one should endure such turmoil, especially a child. A child should only worry about what kind of cookie he or she is allowed to have for a snack. A child should only have to worry about what color barrettes or socks to wear to school. What toy he or she wants for his or her birthday. Not be too afraid to get on and off the school bus and sit in a classroom full of bullies.

Society has blinded us all. It has made us believe that being beautiful is *skinny, long hair, fair skin* and *being superficial*. I beg to differ!

What happened to loving one's self? What happened to knowing one's self-worth, and being a good person, helping others, and having compassion? I guess those things vary from each individual! It's sad that we live in a world where what brand names someone wears, or what kind of car he or she drive determines how they are treated in society. It is time to wake up people! Wake up before our next generation of leaders repeat the cycle instead of break it.

I have spent years trying to fit in only to find out that I was created different for a reason. God did not create us the same. Sure we may have similar qualities, but each person has been blessed with their own purpose in life. It is simply up to us to figure out that purpose.

I was not always confident in speaking my mind, but I thank God for growth. I think God for deliverance. I thank God for helping me find myself, love myself, and never allow another person on this beautiful planet cause me to put down on myself and others. I could go on and on about my life and all that I have conquered but for now, I want to talk about something that was severely painful for me growing up. I know many people, especially girls, will be able to relate in some form or fashion. I pray that you are blessed by my testimony.

I am Harmony Renee Jackson, and this is my hair journey.

Chapter 1
Mommy It Hurts

Harmony walked into her parent's bedroom while her mother was reading and her father was busy taking a shower. She rubbed her little eyes to keep the tears from impairing her vision.

"Mommy, my hair hurts. I have sores in my head. Can you look at it please?"

At only five years old, Harmony was mature than most kids her age, her mother noticed. She told her that because she was a big girl, it was time she got rid of the *nappy* hair on her head and become a part of the elite club of *creamy crack goddesses*, in other words, it was time she got her first relaxer.

Now, Rita Jackson was second-guessing herself each time her daughter complained about how much her hair hurt.

"Harmony, get over here! What did I tell you about all that whining and crying like a baby? You are not a baby. You are ten years old now. You should be used to what goes along with being beautiful. Be quiet before you disturb your father. I should give you a spanking and send you back to bed. Get over here! Turn around and lean your head back," her mother said forcefully in a low tone glaring at her with contempt.

Harmony did as her mother said. When her mother saw that she was not exaggerating, she gasped. The phrase *"chemical burns"* was an understatement. There on every inch of Harmony's young scalp revealed the secret of her pain covered with puss and scabs. Her mother held her tight. She knew it was her fault as to why her daughter was in obvious pain, but there was nothing she could do about it now. Easing out of the bed, she hugged her child in a warm embrace to comfort her as best she could and then walked her back to her bedroom.

Instructing Harmony to sit on her bed, Rita Jackson walked into the adjoining bathroom. When she returned she had Vaseline and tea tree oil in her hand.

"Sweetheart, we cannot tell Daddy about this, okay. He will not understand that being beautiful is painful. We girls have to stick together and keep this as our secret. Let me make you feel better." Harmony nodded at her mother.

Rita hugged her daughter. Harmony returned her mother's hug. She wanted to stay in her arms forever. She felt safe. She loved her mother and wanted to please her, but she did not like the way her hair felt now that she was getting that *white stuff* put in it.

"I was tired of fighting with your hair to make it look decent. I do not have time to twist and re-twist your hair every day. God forbid if it rains. Do you want me to leave you at home when I go shopping? I bet you would not like that, not one bit. It was time Harmony. You had to grow up. You cannot stay a baby forever. Getting a *perm* was the best thing to do and once you are older, you will understand and love having your hair straight and smooth like everyone else. Having *nappy, kinky, coily* hair is not pretty. If that is how we were to wear our hair, Madame CJ Walker would not have invented the *straightening comb*. There would be no perms. Do you understand?"

"But Mommy, it hurts! When will the pain go away? Every time you take me to Aunt Kema's beauty salon, and Janice puts that *creamy stuff* in my hair it hurts. When I tell her so, she tells me to wait a few more minutes the longer it stays the prettier my hair will be. She then goes to help someone else while I am sitting there on fire. I tried to tell her! Do I really need to put that stuff in my head Mommy? It smells funny."

Rita was tired of hearing her daughter complain. Her mother had done the same thing to her, and her grandmother to her. Now it was time to keep the tradition going with her daughter. Rita could not go more than three weeks without a *touchup*. Getting a *relaxer* was indeed a painful process, but well worth it in the end. She had work in the morning and Harmony's whining was starting to give her a headache. She did not have time for this.

Slap!

Rita hit Harmony and pulled her face to hers with her hand. "Stop it right now! Do you hear me? If you do not be quiet and turn your head around so I can help make it feel better, I am going to give you something to cry about. Do you understand me little girl?"

Harmony caught her sobs in the back of her throat. Crying in front of her mother would only make things worse, and Harmony did not want a whipping.

"I said do you understand me," Rita spoke firmly.

"Yes Ma'am. But..."

"...but nothing. Turn around."

Harmony sat down in front of her mother. When the tea tree oil hit her scalp she nearly wet herself to keep from screaming out in pain. The burning sensation touched the depths of her soul. Harmony prayed in that moment that she would not have to endure anymore pain. It hurt so bad.

After her mother put the Vaseline on her scalp, it began to feel better. It somehow soothed the pain away. Harmony hugged her mother and thanked her for taking care of her pain.

"I know it hurts sometimes Sweetheart, but being a female comes along with great sacrifice. You do not have to worry about all of that now, but some day you will. Boys like girls with *straight hair* they can run their fingers through, Harmony. They do not like *nappy hair* and neither should you. One day you will agree with me, but for tonight just take my word for it. In case you forget in the future, in this house, we perm our hair not wear it unkempt looking like an animal out of the jungle. Do I make myself clear?"

The look in her mother's eyes was scary. Harmony admitted to herself. She did not want to upset her mother any more than she had already. She nodded her head up and down in agreement.

When Harmony's father came in later to tuck her in bed, she would leave them alone, but not before placing her index finger over her lips to warn Harmony of telling their secret. Nights like this would go on for years.

Harmony cried herself to sleep that night in pain, like so many other nights since she got her first perm. How could her mother do that to her? Harmony prayed, asking God to take her pain away.

Dear God,

I know that I am a child, but I know you can hear me. Please change Mommy's ways. Please make her stop taking me to the beauty salon to get relaxers. They hurt so much, God. I can barely sleep at night because it hurts to lay my head on my pillow. Most nights I sit up in bed because it is the only way I get rest. I am a little girl. I should be playing with my dollies instead of being so unhappy. Amen.

Harmony's prayer was short and sweet. Deep down she knew everything would eventually be okay.

~~~

In the beginning, Harmony was excited to get her first relaxer. She saw her mother with long, shiny, silky hair, and wondered why hers did not look like that. Although she would smile at her curls in the mirror, Harmony still could not understand why her hair looked so different. Harmony loved her curls the way they bounced when she ran and played. She loved the way they felt when she twirled them around her fingers. She loved how her mother put little ribbons and barrettes in her hair when she went to church or school. She loved when her grandmother use to twist her hair in big chucky twists when she went to stay with her, and how her grandmother would let her help her do the same to her own. Yet, Harmony wanted to have hair like her mother. She wanted anything that would please her mother and keep her happy because whenever her mother was not happy, Harmony got the blame and punishment that came along with it. She could not stand to have a sore scalp and a sore behind too so she sucked it up and did what her mother said.

Whenever she went to the beauty salon with her mother, she would see all the women with their hair done the same way and began to wonder why she was so different. It was not until her fifth birthday that Harmony's longing to have hair like her mothers' came into existence. Aunt Kema was out of town the day Harmony experienced her *beauty-milestone*, as her mother called it.

The very first time she smelled the *white stuff* and felt the tingling sensations in her head made her feel like a *big girl*. The day she got her first *relaxer* was bitter-sweet. When her mother saw her, she smiled and told her how pretty she looked, but when they got home and her father saw her he asked what had her mother done to his little girls' beautiful curls. Her grandmother was heartbroken when she went to visit her the following weekend. "What happened to your curls," her Gramps asked with tears in her eyes. "They were so beautiful. I guess we will just have to find something else to do while we are together." Her grandmother was referring to doing their hair together. It was something they did to bond with each other. They would share stories and laughs during that time of Harmony's visits to her grandmother's home.

Harmony felt really sad, but there was nothing she could do to change what had already been done. As long as her mother was happy, nothing else mattered.

"Daddy don't I look beautiful," Harmony recalled asking her father.

"Sweetheart you were beautiful just the way you were. You did not have to change your hair to be beautiful. Do not let anyone tell you otherwise."

Her father's statement made Harmony miss her curls. That night as she took her bath she wondered if her curls would come back if she wet her hair like they did when her mother and grandmother combed her hair. It did not happen the way Harmony had hoped and she received a painful spanking when her mother came to help her out of the tub. Harmony learned a valuable lesson. Having relaxed hair was totally different than having kinky hair.

Her mother had spent a lot of money getting her hair done all pretty and she had ruined it. Rita made Harmony stay in her bedroom that night without eating dinner. She said it would teach her a lesson about wasting money and doing something she had no business doing. Harmony never tried that again.

When Harmony went to school with her long, flowing, *Shirley Temple curls*, as the beautician called them, everyone smiled at her. All the girls wanted to be her friend. They did not ignore her anymore. Harmony finally felt accepted. She fit in with her peers. She did not miss her curls anymore. Not until years later.

Everything was good until she turned ten and her experience with relaxers turned into a nightmare.

"Beauty comes with a price, Harmony. Do not ever forget that."

Those words of her mother would stay with Harmony for the rest of her life, and each day she would try to live up to them which always came with a price. Harmony learned on many occasion that those words did not just apply to outer beauty, but inner beauty as well. In fact, inner beauty was affected much more.

Chapter 2
Covered Scars

Each night, Harmony cried in the comfort of her bedroom in fear that her mother would hear her. Her head hurt and she did not know what to do. Her hair was coming out in patches and she was too afraid to mention it to her parents, especially her mother. School was about to begin so Harmony knew she had to say something. She was going into middle school and the kids were meaner. She did not want to suffer from ridicule. Or feel like a freak show.

"What can we do to hide this mess Janice," Harmony's mother asked their beautician.

"Rita, this child needs to go see a doctor. Her scalp is irritated awfully bad. Her hair is falling out and I will not give her another relaxer. You need to stop this and take her to see a doctor. I was against giving her a perm at the age of five anyway, which is probably the reason you brought her here when you knew Kema would be out of town at a hair show. She was too young and since you did not bother to take care of her hair the way you should have, she is suffering from it. Does Jason know about this?"

"Please do not worry about what *my husband* knows Janice! Mind your business and do as I am paying you to do."

Rita shifted her weight from one side to the other. She knew she was in trouble. Her daughter's hair was a mess and sadly, it was her own fault. No, she did not wrap it up at night or style it the next morning. She did not wash it and comb it as she should have. She had to work plus take care of the household. That is why she got Harmony a perm in the first place. She needed something to help her manage her thick, nappy locs. Now, looking at her child's hair, Rita felt sick to her stomach. Once upon a time she had simply adored Harmony's curls. But jealousy got the best of her and now her daughter was suffering because of it.

"Look Janice, I need your help. I am sorry for raising my voice. Can you at least braid it or something? She starts school on Monday. I promise to schedule an appointment for her to see a doctor next week. Please do not make my baby go to school with her hair looking like this. Please, Janice!"

"This is wrong on so many levels, Rita. You are wrong! If Kema finds out about this, I can lose my station here. This will be the last time I can do you or your daughter's hair."

Harmony listened at the two women go back and forth over her hair. She wanted to run away.

After about twenty minutes, her beautician Ms. Janice took her back to the wash bowl and soothed her scalp as best she could. Afterwards, she gave her a deep conditioning and hot oil treatment. "This will help with the breakage, Sweetie."

Harmony looked at the sadness in Ms. Janice's eyes. She knew at this point, nothing would help her hair or lack thereof. The only good thing for her was that she had very thick hair so many of the patches could be camouflaged.

After Ms. Janice came to rinse her hair and take her back up front to her personal working station, Harmony wanted to go home. They had been at the salon all day. She was tired, hungry, and ready to see her daddy. He would make her feel better.

Ms. Janice worked her magic. When she turned the chair around to face the mirror, Harmony could not help but smile. Her hair looked amazing. It was longer than she remembered and there were no patches anywhere. Needless to say, Harmony had received her first sew-in weave and did not know it. That night when she got home and the pain from her hair being too tight kicked in, she knew something was different. When she asked her mother, she was told to be quiet and go to her room until dinner was prepared. Her mother did give her two aspirin before shushing her away.

Harmony called her best friends Erica and Kelly and told them what she suspected.

"Girl, I wish my Momma would let me get a weave. You are so lucky! I bet when we get to school on Monday everyone will want to be your friend because of your hair. Do you like it? Is it long or short? Curly or straight?"

Harmony told her friends about her new hair. The only person excited about it was Kelly. Harmony and Erica must have made her unhappy about not being so enthused about the weave because she quickly decided to get off the phone. "Anyway, I have to go. See you at school," said Kelly.

She and Erica were closer so Harmony was able to confide in her. She knew Erica would never betray her; however, Kelly was a different story. Not knowing that Kelly was still on the phone listening in, Harmony's life was about to change again.

That would not come until later, but the true meaning of friendship was not something Kelly prided herself in maintaining or cared too much about when it came to getting what she wanted.

~~~

The first day of middle school was awesome, Harmony thought on her way home. She and Erica walked to and from school each day. They had been best friends since nursery school. Erica had been right. Everyone saw her hair and immediately wanted to be her friend. But, Harmony was so focused on Erica's hair that she did not care. Her best friend's hair was beautiful. The big, thick, and curly mane on top of her head looked surreal. Harmony had to touch it to see if it were real. "What did you do to your hair?"

"My Momma said I could wear it out on the first day of school. Then the braids go back in," Erica said. "I did not even know it had gotten this huge until she took my braids down a few weeks ago to put more in. I have worn braids so long. I just figured she was trying to make me look decent because I did not have any hair. Well, as everyone can see, I have more than enough."

"Yes you do! It is gorgeous, Erica. Your mom does not perm your hair?"

"Oh goodness no, Harmony, we wear our hair in its natural state. My mom says it is how we were born, and it should be our way of life until the day we die. I embrace my natural hair, Harmony. I can wear it anyway I want; however, we are still kids so I have to wear my braids. My sisters wear their hair in twists, in fros, straight and in any other way they decide. They always have some kind of fresh, cute, funky style. One of my sisters uses beautiful scarves and wraps. She is in college so she is not confined to wear it the way others think she should. I cannot wait to be able to do that."

"Well, my mom says that getting a relaxer is beautiful. She says that boys like girls with straight hair instead of nappy hair."

Erica smiled. "Who made your mom the Queen of speaking for all the boys? My dad and my brothers love the way my mom, my sisters, and I wear our hair.

What does your dad say about the way you wear your hair Harmony?"

Harmony thought for a second. She knew her father did not approve of her getting relaxers. She knew it was the reason her mother told her to never mention being taken to the beauty salon, or the sores and scalp irritations. Harmony knew keeping their secret was wrong, and would later pay for it deeply.

When they saw Kelly at school that day, she avoided them. She had a certain look on her face. Harmony should have known nothing good would come from being friends with Kelly, but she overlooked it when Kelly showed up at her house that evening.

"Let me see it," Kelly asked.

"See what?"

"Don't play dumb with me Harmony. I was still on the phone last night when you and Erica were talking. I know about your little secret and if you do not let me see, I am going to tell everyone at school tomorrow."

Harmony did not know what to say or do, so she showed Kelly her tracks. Sure she told them about her speculation of having a weave, but she never wanted anyone to know for sure. Now that Kelly did, Harmony knew she had to be careful. Kelly wasn't to be trusted. She had betrayed friends before.

"That is so cool Harmony. I wonder if I can get my hair like that, wearing ponytails is starting to get old. We are getting much older and soon we will be in high school. I cannot wear ponytails in high school."

"Your hair looks beautiful Kelly."

What happened next was beyond Harmony's wildest dream. Kelly removed the bobby pins from her hair and took out her ponytail.

"See, it isn't real. You are not the only one dealing with your hair Harmony. At least your mother can afford to take you to the salon. My mother cannot. And because of that my hair doesn't grow."

That night, Kelly and Harmony became closer. They had something in common they had no intentions of even sharing with anyone else, not even Erica.

Chapter 3
Friends & Enemies

Harmony and Erica remained friends over the years. Kelly, not so much. Her hair started to grow and she blossomed into a beautiful social butterfly. She no longer needed them anymore. She became the easy chick that all the boys friended just to get inside her pants. Too bad Kelly was so wrapped up in her beauty she did not see it coming until it was too late. She ended up pregnant not knowing who the father was, and so embarrassed that she dropped out of school. However, not before she took a few people with her down the road of unpoplarity.

When they got to high school, Harmony was wearing wigs due to having all of her hair fall out from the sew-ins. They were too tight and her hair already being in a fragile state, could not take it. Erica had been there when she was teased at school when one of her tracks came out during lunch. The kids were horrible to her and Erica was the only one to stand up for her and remain by her side.

During that time of her life, Harmony wanted to end it all. She would have if her father had not come home the day she tried to hang herself in her bathroom. Just as she was about to step off the side of the tub, her father called her name somehow bringing her back to reality. Harmony promised herself that she would never think about or attempt hurting herself again. Never in a million years could she have ever guessed her life would be so dreadful at such a young age. Thanks to Ms. Janice who took her under her wing, shaved her head bald, and helped her start over.

Harmony was able to blend in and keep a low profile until Kelly gave her the limelight.

Who knew boys could cause the best of friends to turn on each other? Well, Kelly was infatuated with a boy who liked Harmony. Harmony did not like him in the least and told Kelly so, but whenever she saw him talking to Harmony; Kelly became insane.

One day during lunch, in front of everyone, Kelly approached Harmony and Erica as they sat together eating fries. Before anyone knew what was happening, Kelly quickly pulled off Harmony's wig and walked it over to the guy and threw it in his face. "Is this what you want? That baldheaded hoe! Do you like her now?"

Harmony ran away with tears streaming down her face. Erica was right there behind her. Kelly laughed with everyone else. The joke would be on her in a few short months, though.

Harmony told her mother what happened. Her mother called Kelly's mother and they had words. Harmony knew in that moment she and Kelly would never be friends again. She missed school for a month, taking online classes to not get behind in her studies. Her mother said this would give everyyone a chance to calm down and forget about what happened. It would also give them time to figure out a way to make everyone not think about what happened. While Harmony was out of school, her hair grew back. This is when Harmony got introduced to *hair infusion*.

Hair infusion is simply a technique to add hair extentions that strands a synthetice or human hair texture to a person's own natural hair folicilles with a glue adhesive, without anyone knowing the difference. It was expensive, but Harmony's mother wanted her to be comfortable and liked at school. She also wanted her daughter to be beautiful, just like her.

Too bad her mother's definition of what beautiful was made her little girl a target of manipulation and blackmail, accompanied with low self-esteem.

When Harmony got home from the salon with her hair infusion, she loved it. It looked real. It was not too short or too long. No one would know it wasn't her own hair. Life was starting to brighten for Harmony. Being a high school student was about to change for her and for the better.

~~~

Harmony started to envy and resent Erica with all the attention she got from everyone over her hair. She had to admit, Erica's hair had grew longer and thicker. She now wore it big and proudly. Sure, Harmony received compliments on her hair but she knew she was living a lie. Erica never told her secret about the wigs and Harmony never shared her secret with Erica about the hair infusion. She wanted it to stay that way. Kelly had taught her a valuable lesson in friendship and keeping secrets. Even though Harmony knew Erica would never hurt her like Kelly, she simply could not take any chances.

Her mother hardly spoke to her unless it was time to revamp her extensions or go shopping. She did not care about how she was doing in school just as long as she looked good and stayed out of her way. She did not see Harmony's insecurities and low self-esteem. She turned a blind eye and ear to the sadness on her face and the tears running down her cheeks.

Even though Harmony kept her grades up, she was fighting to stay alive. She was too afraid to live in fear that her secret would be revealed; therefore, she never dated or went anywhere if it was not with Erica. Now that Erica was seriously dating and actively involved in sports, they did not spend as much time together.

Harmony focused all of her attention on her studies in hopes that when she graduated from high school, she would be able to get as far away from her hometown as possible. She ran into Kelly a few times, but never said anything to her. She now had two kids by two different guys, but still did not know which two guys out of the many she slept around with were the fathers.

Harmony's parents had gotten a divorce years ago due to the many issues they tried to keep hidden. It was for the best, Harmony concluded. She was happy to be free of all the arguing that went along with her parents being under the same roof.

Where had the love gone? What changed along the years that pulled her family apart? Whenever she asked questions, both of her parents told her not to worry about it. They assured her it was not her fault and left it at that. Somehow, deep down inside, Harmony thought differently.

Harmony kept getting hair infusions until her own hair grew back. She took out the extensions in hope's that her mother would allow her to wear her own hair once and for all, but was quickly told it wasn't long enough. It was not beautiful enough. Harmony was crushed. Why was she not enough for her mother? When would she ever be good enough for her mother? Would she ever be good enough for her mother?

Harmony went right back to the weaves. Ms. Janice refused to do her hair anymore, so Harmony and her mother found another salon who would.

Once she was able to stop worrying about someone discovering her secret, Harmony came out of her shell. She and Erica lived it up during their last two years of high school. She began dating a guy name Nicolas, a friend of Erica's boyfriend Trey. They were happy until she completely forgot about her secret and it became exposed; a silent killer of her soul.

Chapter 4
Innocence Lost

Getting hair infusion became too much for Harmony. With her studies, being a part of various school organizations, and doing community outreach, she did not find the necessary time to get her hair done as she should have in order to maintain it properly. And after her own hair grew back, she did not feel the need to take care of it as she should have. Deep down, her scalp was untreated and the problem was about to strike hard.

Harmony noticed strands of hair falling out when she washed her hair. This went on for months before she decided to say something. She tried telling her mother, but was told not to mention anything regarding her hair again.

Her mother called her names and said she should just grow up already. Harmony wanted hair like her mothers'. Even though she knew her mother wore hair extensions, they looked real. They looked perfect on a daily basis and Harmony wondered why her own was not like that. They went to the same salon, although she never witnessed her mother getting her hair done. Harmony felt helpless. Would she ever make her mother proud of her appearance?

Harmony became so stressed out about her hair that she began experiencing breakouts all over her body. She went from one doctor to the next. She spent thousands of dollars on product after product, only to be told years later that her condition had nothing to do with stress. The breakouts stemmed from all the chemicals from the years of getting relaxers, which got into her bloodstream. Who knew hair and the way one chose to wear it could play such a huge part in one's health?

She had had enough. Harmony decided to get rid of the hair extensions and return to wearing wigs. After she wanted to get braids and her mother told her no, she had no other choice. Her body was suffering immensely. Everyone stared when she entered a room or walked around school. Harmony found herself staying inside most days even when the weather was beautiful. She could not chance an encounter with another rude and heartless person. In the dead of summer, Harmony was always covered from head to toe to keep her breakouts concealed.

Her father still did not know she was keeping this secret, although he had speculation. He noticed the sadness whenever they spent time together. Whenever they went on vacation to the beach, Harmony never wore a swimsuit. She never got in the water or took off any of the layers of clothing she came accustomed to wearing. Her father tried asking about the different hair styles she wore, but Harmony always changed the subject. They instead talked about academics, colleges, sports, things that were leading society to damnation.

Harmony was intrigued by her fathers' knowledge. He was the most brilliant man she knew. His laugh was infectious. No matter how low she felt, when she heard his laughter, her world was alright again. Harmony adored her father to no end.

The wigs Harmony wore looked so real at times she forgot. She spent hundreds of dollars on them. She took them to the beauty salon and let Janice style them for her. They had become good friends over the years.

It was not until her senior year of high school that Harmony's secret was exposed.

~~~

Harmony and Nicolas became inseparable. They had been dating now for two years. They did everything together. He became her best friend, even though she and Erica still hung out and talked on the phone daily. Nicolas made her feel special, accepted, and normal. He told her how beautiful she is. The only other male to say those words to her was her father, so Harmony felt delightful. She could finally have a normal life.

The talk about what happened between her and Kelly eventually went away. Since Nicolas did not attend their school at that time, Harmony was glad. He did not know what went down. At ease he never mentioned it to her if he did. He was not the type of person to listen or entertain gossip. He reminded her of her father in that way too.

Nicolas met her parents and they adored him. After being divorced for two years, her parents began dating again and got remarried. They were happier than Harmony ever remembered seeing them. Pleased to have her family back intact, Harmony knew this time around would be better for them all. She saw this as a sign from God as a new beginning. If only that applied to her hair, Harmony thought day in and day out.

She shared everything with Nicolas except her hair secret, which she was not too sure about doing. She had to feel him out more. Two years was not enough time to divulge every secret in Harmony's mind. It took more time than that to truly discover the nature of one's character. She could not afford to have it come back to punch her in the face like Kelly. Harmony still wondered how someone who called themselves a *friend* could betray another in the worse way. She would never know because she did not ever plan on speaking to or being in Kelly's company again.

One night, after attending a movie, they went back to Nicolas's house. His parents were out of town. Things began to move rapidly, and Harmony found herself in a sticky situation. Nicolas kissed her. He told her he loved her, all of her, no matter what. She was not ready to go all the way, but she wanted Nicolas to like her. As things got more intense Harmony felt her wig shift. Before she could do anything it came off of her head exposing her patchy hair and irritated scalp. She pushed Nicolas away and tried to get up. He forced her back down.

"Where do you think you are going you baldheaded hoe? Everyone said you wore wigs, but I thought they were just messing with me. My own blood tried to warn me, but I did not listen. See, Kelly is my cousin. She told me about you a long time ago, and we plotted to ruin you for getting her kicked out of school."

Harmony could not believe her ears. "I had nothing to do with Kelly leaving school. She dropped out because she got pregnant not because of me. She told you a lie! Nicolas, let me up. I want to go home. Please!"

"Shut up! You are nothing, but a liar. I hate liars, and to think I was starting to have real feelings for you. Harmony, I liked you. I thought we had a special bond. I thought you would share your secret with me, but I guess I was not that important. Girls are much worse than guys when it comes to feelings and expressing those feelings. You guys try to make us think it's us. How could you lead me on Harmony?"

Harmony did not know what to say or do. How dare Nicolas try to turn this around on her! How dare he try to make her out to be the bad person in this!

"Nicolas, I do not know what you are talking about. Whatever games you and Kelly are into, I do not want to be a part of them. I have better things to do. I thought you were special and I truly liked you. How could you do this to me? Please, let me up!

"Oh no, I am calling all the shots here. Now, if you want your little secret to remain just that you will do as I say. I have spent two years with you and it will not be for nothing. You owe me!"

That night Harmony got her innocence taken in order to keep her secret hidden. She wanted to die. She wanted to run away and never look back, but instead she allowed Nicolas access to her treasure and cried the entire time. He did not even offer to drive her home afterwards so she walked across town, in pain. When she got home she was happy her parents were asleep. She did not want to explain what happened nor lie to them. Harmony showered that night as the sound of the water shielded her cries. It was a Friday, a night she would never forget. She was just glad there were two days before she had to face Nicolas again.

When she got to school on Monday Nicolas was waiting for her. He held her hand and they walked into school as if nothing ever happened. He kissed her when he walked her to class and whispered in her ear, "you are too sweet, I think I want some more."

Harmony was is total disbelief. She was horrified. That was the day she lost herself. Her self-esteem went out the window. Her confidence soon followed along. Her smile kissed her face for the last time, with no hope of ever returning. Harmony became a walking zombie. She did not care how she looked or dressed. She tried making herself less attractive as possible hoping that Nicolas would finally leave her alone. He blackmailed her the entire year, leaving her broken.

~~~

Graduation came and went and Harmony was ready to go off to college. She received a full-scholarship to a university far away from where she grew up. Nicolas threatened to tell everyone her secret if she did not do as he said. Harmony's senior year in high school became her worst nightmare. They attended prom together, every dance together. She had to go to all of his games and cheer for him. When she was not studying or at school, all of her spare time had to be spent with him. Sex became a part of their routine. He used her to get what he wanted, in order for her secret to stay hidden. Harmony knew it was wrong, but what else could she do? Who could she tell? Her parents were too busy being newlyweds that they barely noticed her at all.

The day before she left for college Harmony was so excited. She spent time with Erica, her parents, and per his request Nicolas. The next day when she got up ready to leave behind the life that had plagued her so bad. Her parents cried when they took her to the airport. They were driving to bring the rest of her things.

~~~

Harmony got comfortable in her seat waiting on the person who would sit next to her to arrive. She closed her eyes and thanked God for finally getting her away from all the hell she had endured during her childhood phase. When she looked up, there standing in front of her was the most amazing person she had ever seen. She looked exotic in her colorful clothing. Her hair was beautiful, in an enormous twist out. Her makeup was flawless and her voice was one of the kindest she had ever heard.

She and the woman, whose name was Imani, talked for hours on the plane. They bonded and Harmony gained a new sense on respect, love, and acceptance of herself. Imani's words gave her the power she needed to finally stand up and be who she knew she could be. She did not feel ashamed, empty, or regretful about the decision she had made. Harmony decided that she would no longer hide behind a wig or weave or extension, nor allow others to dictate her existence again or determining what she should look like. That evening when the plane landed and she found her dorm room, Harmony went to the nearest barber shop and did the *big chop*. She immediately felt free. That day, Harmony took control over her life.

When her parents made it with the rest of her things, her father looked relieved and her mother looked petrified. She told her parents that she had to live life pleasing to herself and to God. That cutting her hair was restoration for her. She told them about everything she had experienced, even what happened with Nicolas. They wanted to have him arrested, but Harmony was ready to let that part of her past die. It took much convincing, but Harmony was finally able to keep her parents from going to the police, over to his house, and beating the crap out of him. *It would have been fun watching*, Harmony thought to herself.

"Mom, Dad. I have lived to please others all of my life until now. I had to do this for me. I was dying, floating in a sea of loneliness, but never again. I am finally *free*. This has nothing to do with anyone but me. In order for me to be happy, I have to first be happy with who I am. I never understood it before but I do now. Please understand. If you cannot, I apologize; however, this is who I am now. It's spiritual for me. Being my natural self is being the best me I can be. God created me this way and this feels so right. I loved my curls when I had them, and because I wanted to be like you, Mom, I let them go. They are a part of me. I am not saying having straight relaxed hair is not beautiful. I am merely saying it is not the way I was meant to wear my own."

Her parents nodded in agreement with her. They embraced her trying to take all the pain away that she had suffered. Harmony released years of pent up emotion. She cleansed in her parents' arms. She exhaled.

The next morning she and her parents went to have breakfast. They helped her with anything she needed them to. Harmony noticed on that particular day, as she walked with her parents with her head up high, she received many smiles and nods from people. She even noticed a few good-looking guys admiring her natural beauty. Her father must have noticed too because Harmony heard him mumble *"I hope I do not have to come back with my gun."* Harmony and her mother laughed to themselves. They enjoyed a nice dinner that evening and laughed until their stomachs hurt. It was a time neither of them would ever forget.

Harmony hugged her parents before they had to leave and return home on the next day. She cried tears of joy knowing that her life would never be the same. It was not until she heard whispers as she walked to class her first day of college that she began to doubt her decision, but someone called her name. It was Erica, her best friend.

As it turns out, Erica wanted to surprise Harmony by not telling her they would be attending the same school. When Erica saw Harmony's hair, she beamed like the sun. "Well it's about damn time! I have waited so long for this day. You look absolutely gorgeous Harmony. Do not let anyone tell you differently."

Harmony knew then, without any doubt, that she had made the right decision. She rubbed her hand across her smooth head and smiled. *It is only hair, it will grow back!*

Chapter 5
A Fresh Do

As months went by, Harmony loved her decision to cut her hair more each day. Her hair began to grow back and she got back the beautiful, thick, spiral curls she loved as a child. She experimented with twists, braids, head wraps, and just letting her hair be free. She learned in her African-American Studies class the way women wore their hair determined their social status, their level of power or confidence, and how they saw themselves among their peers.

Harmony was intrigued by all the knowledge she gained. Her professor spoke highly of natural hair and how it was not for everyone, but individuals who loved themselves internally. Harmony saw that many of her classmates both male and female wore their hair in its natural state. She admired all the beauty surrounding her. It felt good being in the midst of great company with like-minded individuals. She became friends with many of them. Her college experience was looking brighter than she could have ever imagined, and having Erica there to share it with was the icing on the cake.

It was not all *easy-breezy* for Harmony because some days she missed her long flowing hair. It helped shield her low self-esteem that was slowly returning, or other flaws she carried each day from outsiders. It helped make her feel normal, but what is normal? Does the way one wears their hair make them normal? Does the way one dress makes them normal?

Harmony concluded that it was a little bit of both. The more she looked in the mirror and began to love the person staring back at her she remembered Imani's words, *"Stop putting so much energy into people who do not know you, and start putting that energy into the person who know you best, yourself."*

Those words changed something inside of her. Those words helped Harmony see the bigger picture, in color. They helped her truly understand the phrase, *"how can someone else love you when you do not love yourself?"*

Harmony made a total transformation. She was no longer a victim. She was no longer afraid to be herself. She was no longer silenced to the things she was passionate about and voicing her opinion propelled her into the next phase of her purpose. She had Erica to show her different products and techniques that worked amazing for natural hair.

Harmony learned that what she put into her body, reflected in her hair. If she did not drink enough water, her hair revealed it to her by the way it felt and looked. It became brittle with more shrinkage and lacked volume. Harmony discovered that although Erica's hair loved almond oil, it was not necessarily the case for her own. It was too heavy for her hair and made her hair limp. Harmony learned that coconut oil was not only good for cooking, but that it made her hair shiny, moisturized, and easy to twist. She learned that if she did not fully let her twists dry before taking them down, she would look like a *chia pet* the next day.

Harmony met other peers, who became new friends that wore their hair in its natural state, and learned new tricks and information from them all. It was like a new language. It was educational. It was a life-changing experience, and one Harmony deeply loved and cherished. It was a part of who she is and would forever be.

The more knowledge Harmony learned about her natural hair, the more she embraced it. The more her hair grew, the more confident she became, and her past washed away.

Harmony learned how to do amazing hair styles for any occasion. It was not true at all that people with natural hair looked unkempt, unprofessional, and uneducated. She received many compliments whenever she attended an event or went off with the debate team for a competition. It was people and their ignorance to a particular person, place, or thing that they did not understand and could not identify with that formed so many stereotypes and categories they placed others in.

It's a shame we live in a world that judges other's by what they think should or should not be acceptable.

Harmony no longer needed validation from others. She was alright with herself and that was all that mattered. If she gained a compliment, new friend, or valuable lesson along her journey so be it! However, it was not going to stop her from living, instead of just existing in a life of regret.

Harmony used her experience to pour into the lives of others. She volunteered at a youth home and spoke to young boys and girls about peer pressure, staying true to themselves, and living life with purpose.

A few of the kids loved her hair and some did not. It no longer mattered to Harmony, but she wanted her message from her personal testimony to help them have brighter futures. She worked with the group of kids until they graduated from the program, and then worked with the new ones who came afterwards. Harmony was determined to live with purpose and help others figure out their passion so they could discover their own.

Chapter 6
Learning to LOVE me

"Look at her nappy headed ass. She needs to buy a wig or something."

"She needs to get a damn perm! Why would you want your hair to be nappy when it does not have to be?"

"It looks okay."

"No man will ever want her with that nappy ass hair on her head."

Harmony heard the whispers, the harsh words spoken, and saw the stirs from the silly individuals as she walked to her table in the student union. She was use to them. It had been months since her *big chop* and the same people who said hurtful things then, were the same ones saying them now. *Some people will never grow up,* Harmony thought. She put her ear buds in and listened to the words of Dr. Maya Angelou.

Pretty women wonder where my secret lies.
I'm not cute or built to suit a fashion model's size
But when I start to tell them,
They think I'm telling lies.
I say,
It's in the reach of my arms
The span of my hips,
The stride of my step,
The curl of my lips.
I'm a woman
Phenomenally.

Phenomenal woman,
That's me.

I walk into a room
Just as cool as you please,
And to a man,
The fellows stand or
Fall down on their knees.
Then they swarm around me,
A hive of honey bees.
I say,
It's the fire in my eyes,
And the flash of my teeth,
The swing in my waist,
And the joy in my feet.
I'm a woman
Phenomenally.
Phenomenal woman,
That's me.

Men themselves have wondered
What they see in me.
They try so much
But they can't touch
My inner mystery.
When I try to show them
They say they still can't see.
I say,
It's in the arch of my back,
The sun of my smile,
The ride of my breasts,
The grace of my style.
I'm a woman
Phenomenally.
Phenomenal woman,
That's me.

Now you understand

Just why my head's not bowed.
I don't shout or jump about
Or have to talk real loud.
When you see me passing
It ought to make you proud.
I say,
It's in the click of my heels,
The bend of my hair,
The palm of my hand,
The need of my care,
'Cause I'm a woman
Phenomenally.
Phenomenal woman,
That's me.

Such beautiful, inspiring words to live by Harmony acknowledged. She loved poetry, a lover of words, and Dr. Angelou was one of her favorite poets. She gave her encouragement when she did not feel like encouraging herself. Harmony remembered another quote from the amazing woman she adored so much. *"People will forget what you said, people will forget what you did, but people will never forget the way you made them feel."* Harmony wanted to live by Dr. Angelou's words and declared on that day, as she sat alone eating her avocado salad in the student union, that no one would ever make her feel inferior again. No longer would others make her feel unloved, undesired, or unaccepted. No longer would others take advantage of her due to her insecurity.

Harmony now knew the meaning of *self-love, self-respect,* and *self-worth.* She loved who she was and who God created her to become.

Who knew the way she wore her hair could dictate her life in such a way that had her questioning her sanity, her relevance, and her very existence? She would teach her children someday to be themselves, to love themselves, and to live with purpose not the way others thought they should.

Politely, Harmony finished her salad, got up from her table, and walked over to the girls who were saying horrible things about her. They saw her and froze, not knowing what to expect. One was bold, so she spoke first. "Can we help you with something?"

Harmony smiled. "My name is Harmony. If you have a problem with me, there must be something wrong with you. The only people I know who constantly put down on others for talking, walking, wearing their hair a certain way, or dressing a certain way are the ones who are trying hard to keep the spotlight off their own flaws. I lived in silence, in fear, in pain, and unacceptance for years and I refuse to do it again. You do not know me. You have not tried to get to know me, yet here you sit judging me and others. Why? What purpose does this serve? What will you gain? I truly feel sorry for you all!"

"B..."

Before the meanest of the girls sitting at the table was able to finish calling Harmony a nasty word, she cut her off.

"I love me! You do not have to. I live for me! You do not have to. I respect myself! You will too. We may never become friends and I am perfectly okay with that. However, before you judge others, you should really get to know them first."

Harmony turned to walk away, but paused. There was something else she had to say. She faced the girls again. She smiled the brightest smiles looking them each in the eyes. She said...

"AND IF YOU DON'T LIKE MY HAIR... JUST RELAX!"

Harmony walked off with sure radiance. Everyone in the student union that day would forever remember the girl who stood up to ignorance, who possessed such confidence. She did not know it then, but she inspired many people that very day and would continue to inspire others for many years to come.

Stay tuned for more stories about Harmony and her *hair-tales* coming soon in the near future!

About the Author:

Keke Chanel is from the small town of Greensburg, Louisiana. She is a wife and mother, residing in Hammond, Louisiana. Keke began her natural hair journey in 2000. Through trial and error, Keke has maintained a successful path of being natural and loving every minute of it. Keke is the Author of several other books:

Novels:
Deadly In Stilettos
Sugah & Spice (Sugah series)
Naughty or Nice (Sugah series)
Diary of a Misunderstood Brotha
Suffer No More (Suffer series)

Two short-stories:
Passionate Pleasures I
Passionate Pleasures II

For more information about the Author, please visit her website www.thekekechanel.com.